P9-CQJ-982

The Day I Saw My Father Cry

The Day I Saw My Father Cry

by Bill Cosby

Illustrated by Varnette P. Honeywood

Introduction by Alvin F. Poussaint, M.D.

SCHOLASTIC INC.

New York Toronto London Auckland Sydney Mexico City New Delhi Hong Kong

Assistants to art production: Rick Schwab, Nick Naclerio

Library of Congress Cataloging-in-Publication Data

Cosby, Bill, 1937-
       The day I saw my father cry / by Bill Cosby; illustrated by Varnette P. Honeywood.
       p.   cm.— (Little Bill books for beginning readers)
       "Cartwheel books."
       Summary: Although Little Bill is sad when a friend of the family dies, he remembers the friend's lesson of saying "Merry Christmas" to get people to stop fighting.
       ISBN 0-590-52197-7 (hardcover) 0-590-52199-3 (pbk)
       [1. Conduct of life Fiction. 2. Death Fiction. 3. Afro-Americans Fiction.] I. Honeywood, Varnette P., ill. II. Title. III. Series: Cosby, Bill, 1937-   Little Bill books for beginning readers.
PZ7.C8185Dat   2000
[E] — dc 21   99-25076
                                                                                                      CIP
                                                                                                       AC
10 9 8 7 6 5 4 3 2 1   0/0 01 02 03 04 05

Printed in the U.S.A. 23
First printing, January 2000

Dear Parent:

Even happy families have sad times. Usually, parents and children who have warm, loving relationships with each other enjoy a built-in advantage when it comes to managing the stress caused by painful life events. But this story shows that even in families as close-knit as Little Bill's, dealing with the sudden death of a family friend is hard for parents and children alike.

The whole family loves Alan Mills, a neighbor and close friend of Little Bill's father. He's an exceptional man with a special knack for helping angry people solve their problems peacefully, through negotiation and compromise. In fact, he can stop an argument just by saying "Merry Christmas." Something friendly seems to happen to people when they say (or hear) those words.

When Alan suddenly dies from a heart attack, Little Bill's father is deeply grieved. It's the first time his son has ever seen him cry. But instead of trying to hold back his tears and act tough, the way old-fashioned fathers often used to, he shares his sorrow with his son, and Little Bill learns that it's natural to cry when your heart is broken.

He also discovers that even though Alan is gone, his memory and spirit have stayed with his friends. When Little Bill and his brother get into an argument over whose turn it is to lie on the couch to watch television, they suddenly find themselves employing Alan's wisdom. Instead of getting caught up in a pointless fight (and missing their TV show), they stop themselves by saying "Merry Christmas" to each other. And just saying those words makes them feel so much better, they're able to figure out a way to share the couch. Alan Mills has left an important legacy, and it's a fitting tribute to his values and his life.

Alvin F. Poussaint, M.D.
Clinical Professor of Psychiatry,
Harvard Medical School and
Judge Baker Children's Center,
Boston, MA

*For as they said, it was a shame to quarrel upon
Christmas Day. And so it was! God love it, so it was!*
—*A Christmas Carol*
by Charles Dickens

Chapter One

Hello, friend. I'm Little Bill. One evening, as my family was finishing supper, the doorbell rang.

"Hello, pal," I heard Dad say. "What can I do for you?"

"I'm your new neighbor, Alan Mills. I live across the street in the blue house."

"I'm Bill," said Dad. "Come on in and have a cup of coffee with me and my wife."

Mom rolled her eyes up. "Your father," she whispered. I could see that she wasn't in the mood for company just then.

When Dad and Alan Mills came into the kitchen, my brother Bobby and I said hello to our new neighbor and went to our rooms.

I started to study for a spelling test. Bobby was playing music—loud music.

I had to shout out my spelling words to hear myself think. Noise—n-o-i-s-e. The music got louder. I shouted louder. N-O-I-S-E. The music got even louder.

spelling

I went into Bobby's room and shut off the CD player. But I forgot that I didn't have to shout anymore, so what I said came out very loud. "I CAN'T LEARN MY SPELLING WORDS WITH ALL THIS NOISE, YOU IDIOT!"

And my brother shouted, "YOU CAN'T LEARN YOUR SPELLING WORDS BECAUSE YOU'RE THE IDIOT!"

He was shouting in my face and poking my chest with his finger. So I pulled it, and he screamed that I broke his finger. Then he pushed me, and I pushed him, and before I knew what was happening, we were wrestling on the floor. One of us was bleeding, and three grown-ups were standing above us.

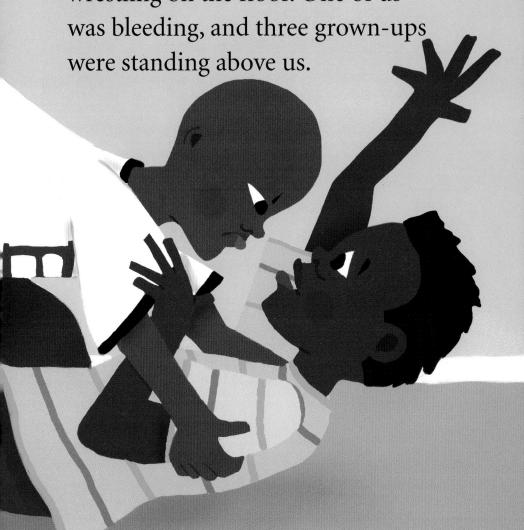

I didn't hear what Mom and Dad were saying, but I did hear when Alan Mills said, "Merry Christmas!"

Bobby and I stopped fighting. It was Bobby's nose that had been bleeding.

"It's not Christmas," Bobby said.

"Yeah, it's not Christmas," I said.

"I know," our neighbor said. "Saying 'Merry Christmas' makes people feel good. So Merry Christmas…pretend it's Christmas. Merry Christmas…think about why you are fighting. Merry Christmas…think about why you are angry. Merry Christmas…think about a better way to solve the problem."

"Like getting Bobby to turn off his music," I said.

"Like getting Little Bill out of my room so I can have some privacy," Bobby said.

"Good ideas!" said Alan. Then he turned to Dad. "I've got some headphones at home. Is it okay if I go get them and lend them to Bobby?"

"Sure," said Dad.

"Then Bobby will be able to hear his music, and Little Bill will be able to hear himself think," Alan said.

So we had a Merry Christmas, even though it was really the end of January! And from that day on, Alan and my dad were very good friends.

Chapter Two

One day in the spring, Michael, Andrew, José, and I were playing two-on-two in the park: José and Michael against Andrew and me. The game was a close one. We were tied until Michael rebounded the ball, dribbled back, and made a basket.

"That doesn't count," Andrew said. "You didn't take it all the way out."

"Yes, I did," Michael said.

"NO, YOU DIDN'T!" Andrew said.

Andrew pushed Michael. Michael pushed Andrew. And our basketball game turned into a wrestling match.

A voice seemed to come from nowhere. "Merry Christmas!"

The fighting stopped. "Hey, it's not Christmas," Michael said.

Alan Mills was standing in front of us. "What happened to that great basketball game I was watching?" he asked.

"Michael didn't take the ball all the way back out to the foul line," said Andrew.

"Yes, I did," Michael said.

"So you boys saw things differently, and then you got angry," said Alan.

"That's right," Andrew said.

"Wouldn't you rather be playing basketball than fighting?" Alan asked.

"Sure," said Michael.

"Then let's cool off, use our brains, and figure something out."

"I think Michael should do it over," Andrew said.

"That would be taking the basket away. That's not fair," said Michael.

"I've got an idea," I said. "This time, we'll decide in Michael's favor. He'll get the points. The next time we disagree, we'll decide in our favor."

"Okay," Michael said.

"It's all right with me," said José.

Andrew picked up the ball. "Me, too," he said. "Let's play some hoops!"

"Merry Christmas," said Alan.

"And Happy Hanukkah, too," said Andrew.

Chapter Three

Coming home from soccer practice one hot summer day, I went to the kitchen to get a glass of water. My dad was sitting with his elbows on the table and his hands on his face.

I went up close to him and saw that he was crying. I had never seen him cry before.

"What's the matter, Dad?" I asked.

My father looked up at me. He pulled me onto his lap and gave me a big hug.

"I'm afraid I have some sad news," said Dad. "Our friend Alan Mills died of a heart attack last night."

My dad and I sat together for a while, quiet and still. "I don't understand," I said. "Alan had such a kind heart. How can someone with such a kind heart get a heart attack?"

"There is the heart and then there's Heart," said Dad. "The heart is a muscle that pumps blood all over the body. 'Heart' has more to do with how a person feels and behaves."

"My heart is broken," I said.

"Mine, too," said Dad.

"Do you remember how Alan Mills always said 'Merry Christmas' to get people to cool off and stop fighting?" I asked.

"I do," said Dad.

"He taught me to do that, too," I said. My dad and I sat and felt sad together.

Chapter Four

The couch in the den was empty. Great. I got there first. I sprawled out on the couch and turned on the TV to watch my favorite show, *Space Explorers,* with Space Captain Zeke.

"GET OFF THAT COUCH!" I heard my brother shout.

"No way," I said. "I was here first."

Bobby shouted back: "I WAS HERE FIRST, THEN I WENT INTO THE KITCHEN TO ANSWER THE PHONE, AND IT WAS THE WRONG NUMBER! SO GET OFF THAT COUCH!"

"THAT'S TOO BAD, AND I WON'T," I said.

Usually, when Bobby and I watch TV, the first one to the couch gets to lie on it. The other has to sit on the couch with feet on his lap.

As far as I was concerned, I got there first. But Bobby had a different opinion. He pulled my arm and my leg until I fell to the ground with a thud and then he spread his body out on the couch. I climbed on top of him and wrestled him to the ground.

Meanwhile, I was missing the first part of *Space Explorers*.

"Merry Christmas," I said.

Bobby and I stopped fighting at the same time.

"Merry Christmas," he said.

"I'll lie down for fifteen minutes. Then you lie down for fifteen minutes," I said.

"I want the first fifteen minutes," Bobby said.

"Okay," I agreed.

As I sat on the couch with my brother's feet on my lap, I felt as if Alan Mills was right there in the room with us.

Bill Cosby is one of America's best-loved storytellers, known for his work as a comedian, actor, and producer. His books for adults include *Fatherhood*, *Time Flies*, *Love and Marriage*, and *Childhood*. Mr. Cosby holds a doctoral degree in education from the University of Massachusetts.

Varnette P. Honeywood, a graduate of Spelman College and the University of Southern California, is a Los Angeles-based fine artist. Her work is included in many collections throughout the United States and Africa and has appeared on adult trade book jackets and in other books in the Little Bill series.

Books in the LITTLE BILL series:

The Best Way to Play: None of the parents will buy the new *Space Explorers* video game. How can Little Bill and his friends have fun without it?

The Day I Saw My Father Cry: It is a very sad day. Little Bill and his father have lost a special friend.

The Day I Was Rich: Little Bill has found a giant diamond and now he's the richest boy in the world. How will he and his friends spend all that money?

Hooray for the Dandelion Warriors!: It's the boys against the girls. But wait! Everybody is supposed to be on the same team!

The Meanest Thing to Say: All the kids are playing a new game. You have to be mean to win it. Can Little Bill be a winner...and be nice, too?

Money Troubles: Funny things happen when Little Bill tries to earn some money.

My Big Lie: Little Bill's tiny fib grew and grew and GREW into a BIG lie. And now Little Bill is in BIG trouble.

One Dark and Scary Night: Little Bill can't fall asleep! There's something in his closet that might try to get him.

Shipwreck Saturday: All by himself, Little Bill built a boat out of sticks and a piece of wood. The older boys say that his boat won't float. He'll show them!

Super-Fine Valentine: Little Bill's friends are teasing him! They say he's *in love*! Will he get them to stop?

The Treasure Hunt: Little Bill searches his room for his best treasure. What he finds is a great big surprise!

The Worst Day of My Life: On the worst day of his life, Little Bill shows his parents how much he loves them. And he changes a bad day into a good one!